I
LUV
SLOCKET

ISBN 978-1-64468-889-2 (Paperback)
ISBN 978-1-64468-890-8 (Digital)

Covenant Books, Inc.
11661 Hwy 707
Murrells Inlet, SC 29576
www.covenantbooks.com

I
LUV
SLOCKET

T.J. Martin

Here is a story based on what's true about a boy who loved something that no one else knew. It all must have started in preschool class with a substitute teacher named Mrs. Snodgrass, but whatever had happened on that very special day would remain a big mystery because she had since moved away.

Tra came home with his hands in his pockets. He pulled them out to show nothing, but he said he had slocket. His parents just smiled with love like before, for they had no clue what he had said or what was in store. Tra tried to explain the best he could, but the more he tried, the less they understood.

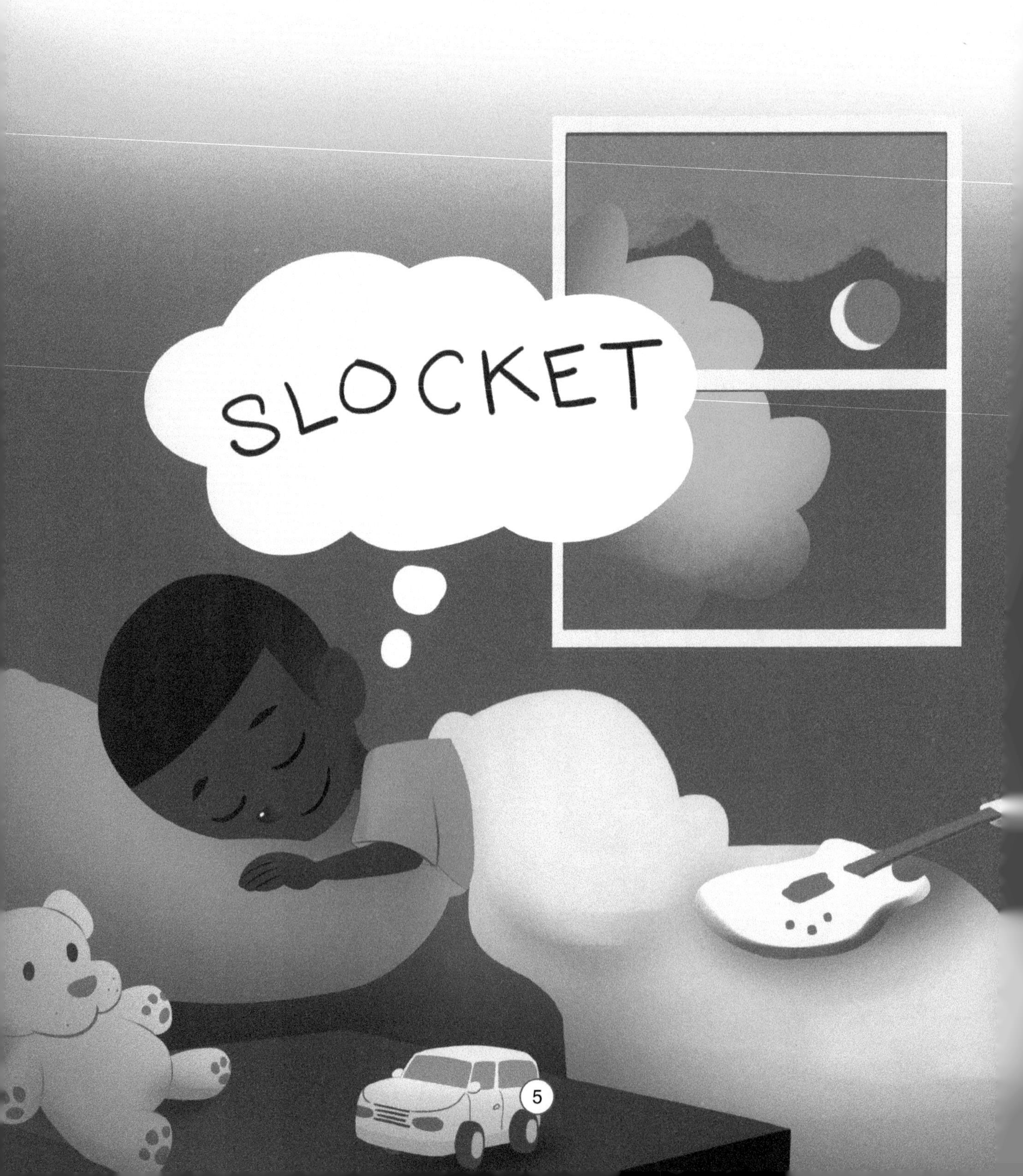
SLOCKET

So to bed he went with a kiss good night. He was tucked in tightly with no slocket in sight. His parents had conquered the word of the day, but tomorrow morning was soon on its way.

Tra woke up that morning and brushed his hair and his teeth.

His mother asked, "What would you like for breakfast?"

Tra replied, "Slocket, please."

Then it was slocket everyday morning, noon, and night. It was slocket at the park while riding his bike. Tra wanted slocket at school, at home, and at church.

What was this slocket driving his parents berserk?

His parents talked to the grandparents, who said it was just a phase. "Give it some time. It will soon pass away."

They talked to the doctor, and the doctor said, "There's no need to worry. It is all in his head."

They took him to church and asked the pastor to pray. He prayed a short prayer and said, "He'll be okay."

And yet it was still slocket after slocket day after day. It was slocket, slocket, slocket…no man could count the number. It was slocket so much that his parents could take it no longer. So that night before Tra went to bed, he was scolded by his father and this is what he said.

"You can never, never, ever, ever say slocket again."

Tra obeyed, and two weeks went by he spoke nothing of slocket. Out of sight out of mind. But then came Saturday, and it was not his intention when he found his baby brother's bottle on the table in the kitchen. Tra tiptoed to his brother not to make a sound, but what he would say in a whisper came out a little too loud. He tried his best to whisper so no one would hear, but the word "slocket" caught his father's ear.

His father ran into the room along with his mother. They asked him excitedly, "What did you say just now to your brother?"

He did not want to repeat what he had said because he might get in trouble and then sent to bed. As he tried to explain with his face full of guilt, he slowly said he asked his brother if he would like some slocket, some slocket milk.

His parents hugged him for now they knew, what Tra was trying to say that no one else knew.

Who in this world would have ever known that slocket was chocolate all along? Perhaps Mrs. Snodgrass.

ABOUT THE AUTHOR

T.J. Martin is a loving father and devoted husband. He has three sons and four grandchildren. His background is in working with at-risk youth. Growing up and seeing his father as a role model to not only him, but to other children prompted him in his own journey of writing his first children's book.

CPSIA information can be obtained
at www.ICGtesting.com
Printed in the USA
BVHW020731240221
600911BV00012B/854

9 781644 688889